by Roger Hargreaves

WORLD INTERNATIONAL

On Monday little Miss Bossy went for a walk.

She met Mr Nosey.

"Where are you going?" he asked.

"Mind your own business," she retorted.

•RETURN THIS WHOLE PAGE•

3 Great Offers For Mr Men Fans

1 FREE Door Hangers and Posters

In every Mr Men and Little Miss Book like this one you will find a special token. Collect 6 and we will send you either a brilliant Mr. Men or Little Miss poster and a Mr Men or Little Miss double sided, full colour, bedroom door hanger. Apply using the coupon overleaf, enclosing six tokens and a 50p coin for your choice of two items.

Egmont World tokens can be used towards any other Egmont World / World International token scheme promotions., in early learning and story / activity books.

Posters: Tick your preferred choice of either Mr Men ☐ or Little Miss ☐

Door Hangers: Choose from: Mr. Nosey & Mr Muddle ☐, Mr Greedy & Mr Lazy ☐, Mr Tickle & Mr Grumpy ☐, Mr Slow & Mr Busy ☐, Mr Messy & Mr Quiet ☐, Mr Perfect & Mr Forgetful ☐, Little Miss Fun & Little Miss Late ☐, Little MIss Helpful & Little Miss Tidy ☐, Little Miss Busy & Little Miss Brainy ☐, Little Miss Star & Little Miss Fun ☐.
(Please tick)

2 Mr Men Library Boxes

Keep your growing collection of Mr Men and Little Miss books in these superb library boxes. With an integral carrying handle and stay-closed fastener, these full colour, plastic boxes are fantastic. They are just £5.49 each including postage. Order overleaf.

3 Join The Club

To join the fantastic Mr Men & Little Miss Club, check out the page overleaf NOW!

Allow 28 days for delivery. We reserve the right to change the terms of this offer at any time but we offer a 14 day money back guarantee. The money-back guarantee does not affect your statutory rights. Birthday and Christmas cards are sent care of parent/guardians in advance of the day. After 31/12/00 please call to check that the offer details are still correct.

•RETURN THIS WHOLE PAGE•

Join Our Club!

MR. MEN & little miss CLUB

When you become a member of the fantastic Mr Men and Little Miss Club you'll receive a personal letter from Mr Happy and Little Miss Giggles, a club badge with your name, and a superb Welcome Pack (pictured below right).

You'll also get birthday and Christmas cards from the Mr Men and Little Misses, 2 newsletters crammed with special offers, privileges and news, and a copy of the 12 page Mr Men catalogue which includes great party ideas.

If it were on sale in the shops, the Welcome Pack alone might cost around £13. But a year's membership is just £9.99 (plus 73p postage) with a 14 day money-back guarantee if you are not delighted!

HOW TO APPLY To apply for any of these three great offers, ask an adult to complete the coupon below and send it with appropriate payment and tokens (where required) to: Mr Men Offers, PO Box 7, Manchester M19 2HD. Credit card orders for Club membership ONLY by telephone, please call: 01403 242727.

To be completed by an adult

❑ **1.** Please send a poster and door hanger as selected overleaf. I enclose six tokens and a 50p coin for post (coin not required if you are also taking up 2. or 3. below).

❑ **2.** Please send __ Mr Men Library case(s) and __ Little Miss Library case(s) at £5.49 each.

❑ **3.** Please enrol the following in the Mr Men & Little Miss Club at £10.72 (inc postage)

Fan's Name:______________________ Fan's Address:______________________________

____

______________________________ Post Code:____________________ Date of birth:___/___/___

Your Name:______________________ Your Address:______________________________

____

Post Code:__________ Name of parent or guardian (if not you):______________________

Total amount due: £________ (£5.49 per Library Case, £10.72 per Club membership)

❑ I enclose a cheque or postal order payable to Egmont World Limited.

❑ Please charge my MasterCard / Visa account.

Card number: | | | | | | | | | | | | | | | | |

Expiry Date: _____/_____ Signature: ______________________

Data Protection Act: If you do **not** wish to receive other family offers from us or companies we recommend, please tick this box ❑. Offer applies to UK only

On Tuesday she met Mr Noisy.

He was singing.

Noisily, of course.

"Shut up!" she told him.

On Wednesday she met Mr Happy.

He was smiling.

As usual.

"Take that silly smile off your face!" she said.

As you can imagine, little Miss Bossy wasn't very popular.

To say the least.

Now, little did Miss Bossy realise, but somebody had seen her bossing Mr Nosey about.

And that same somebody had seen her bossing Mr Noisy about.

And that self-same somebody had seen her bossing Mr Happy about.

The wizard (whose name incidentally was Wilfred) went home, thinking.

"Something really ought to be done about Miss Bossy," he thought to himself as he walked along.

When he arrived home he went straight to his library and took down a large red book from a bookshelf.

It was rather dusty as it hadn't been read for some time.

"Let's see now," he said to himself as he settled into an armchair.

He turned to page three hundred and four.

At the top of the page it said:

'HOW TO STOP PEOPLE BEING BOSSY'.

Wilfred the Wizard read the page very carefully, shut the book, put it back on the bookshelf, and grinned.

A particularly wizardy sort of a grin.

The day after, which was Thursday, little Miss Bossy met somebody who was fast asleep.

As usual.

Mr Lazy.

"Wake up!" she said bossily, and prodded him in the tummy.

"Ouch!" protested Mr Lazy.

But.

Behind Miss Bossy, Wilfred the Wizard, who had been following her, said something too.

Under his breath.

A wizardy word he'd learned from page three hundred and four.

And, do you know what happened?

Suddenly, as if by magic, which is true, there appeared on Miss Bossy's feet a pair of boots.

One minute they weren't there.

The next minute they were.

Miss Bossy looked down in alarm.

They were magic boots and, being magic boots, they could speak to each other.

"Hello Left," said the right boot.

"Hello Right," said the left boot.

"Ready when you are," said Right.

"Right," said Left.

And off they set.

Left. Right. Left. Right. Left. Right. Left. Right.

Faster and faster.

Marching poor little Miss Bossy along.

Little Miss Bossy couldn't do a thing about it.

Mr Lazy was much amused.

"Well done Wilfred," he chuckled.

Wilfred winked a wizardy wink.

Those boots marched little Miss Bossy for five miles.

She was exhausted.

"Ready Left," said the right boot.

"Ready," replied Left.

"Atten...." said Right.

"...shun!" said Left.

And they came to a halt.

Little Miss Bossy was quite out of breath.

She tried to take off her boots.

But it was impossible.

Along came Wilfred.

"Those," said Wilfred, pointing to the boots, "are only for people who are too bossy!"

"Make them go away AT ONCE!" cried Miss Bossy, stamping her foot.

Well, at least she tried to stamp her foot, but the boot wouldn't.

"We're out of stamps," chuckled Right.

Left giggled.

"YOU...WILL...DO...AS...I...SAY!!" shouted Miss Bossy.

"Ready when you are," said Right.

"Right away," replied Left.

"Quick march!"

And off they set again.

Left.

Right.

Left.

Right.

Left.

Right.

For ten miles.

And then they stopped again.

And along came Wilfred.

"MAKE THESE STUPID BOOTS GO AWAY,"
shouted Miss Bossy.

"Only if you say the magic word," replied
Wilfred.

Miss Bossy thought.

And thought.

And thought again.

"Please," she said.

"That's better," smiled Wilfred.

And he said the wizardy word again, under
his breath, from page three hundred and four.

The boots disappeared, as if by magic!

"Now then," said Wilfred sternly, wagging his finger. "Stop being bossy, or you know what will happen."

Miss Bossy nodded.

Miserably.

"Very well," smiled Wilfred.

And went.

And do you know something?

From then on, until now off, little Miss Bossy was a changed person.

Not bossy at all.

And you know why, don't you?

You know what she's afraid of?

Bossyboots!!